Police Officer

Lucy M. George

Ando Twin

Seth is a police officer.

He wears a crisp uniform, with a belt to carry his equipment, a hat, and a badge!

It's Officer Seth's job to protect people in the community.

Officer Seth has an early shift today.
He arrives at the police station right on time!

The sergeant is briefing the team for the day.
"Good morning, Sergeant!" calls Officer Seth.

"Hello, Seth," says the sergeant. Then he gives everyone a job for the day.

Some officers go
out on horseback
to patrol the streets.

Some go to a
crime scene...

...but Officer Seth and
Officer Thea are going
to the local festival!

They go to their police car and check
to make sure everything is working.

Officer Thea tests the special flashing lights
and the siren that makes a loud noise.

Officer Thea drives through the busy
streets on the way to the festival.

Officer Seth keeps an eye on the traffic
to make sure everyone is driving safely.

The festival is busy. People are out in the sun eating, playing games, and enjoying themselves.

Officer Seth and Officer Thea patrol the grounds.

They give a family directions...

...help someone whose car is stuck in the mud...

...and ask a stall worker to keep the path clear.

Suddenly Officer Seth feels a tug on his arm.

It's a little boy.

"I've lost my mom and dad," the boy cries.
"Oh dear," says Officer Seth. "What's your name?"

"Alex," whispers the little boy.
"Don't worry, Alex, we'll find them," says Officer Seth.

Officer Seth asks Alex where he saw his parents last and what they look like.

Then Officer Seth has an idea. "Do you have their phone number?" he asks.

Alex looks in his bag.

"Here!" he says.
"Dad wrote it
down in case of
an emergency."

"Smart Dad!"
says Officer Seth.
He tries calling but
there's no signal.

"We'll never find them!" Alex says.
He starts to cry. He wants his mom and dad.

"Don't worry, Alex, let's try the meeting
point," says Officer Thea. "We will find them!"

As they get close, Alex
thinks he can see his parents...

"Mom! Dad!" Alex cries,
breaking into a run.

"There you are!" says Alex's dad.

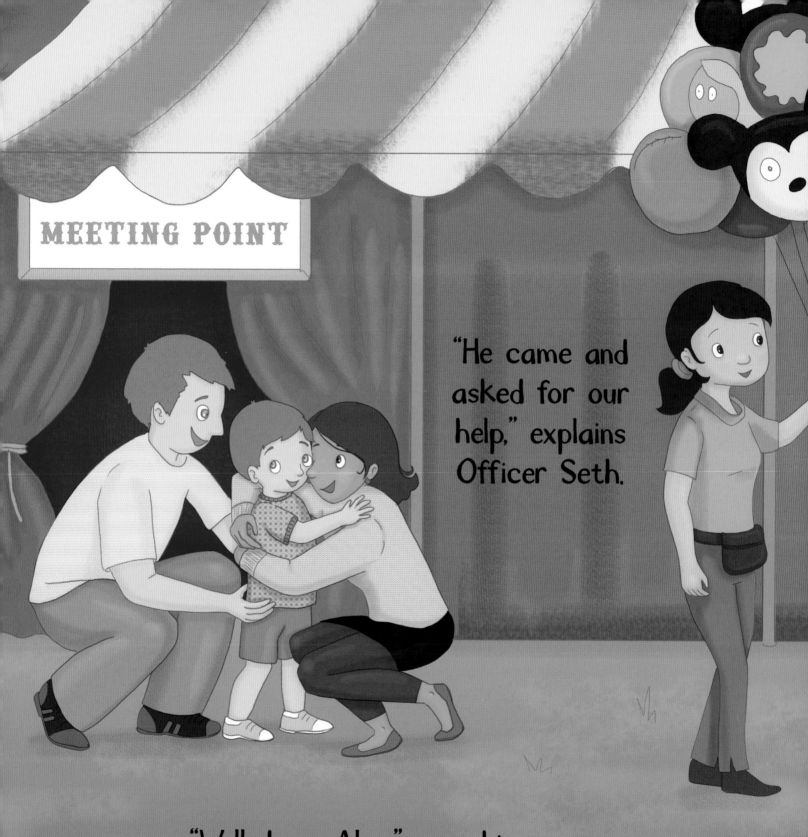

MEETING POINT

"He came and asked for our help," explains Officer Seth.

"Well done, Alex," says his mom.

"Thank you for
helping me,"
Alex says.

"No problem, just doing our job!"
says Officer Seth.

"Enjoy the festival!" says Officer Thea

Officer Seth and Officer Thea decide to get ice cream.

"It's your turn to buy them,"
says Officer Thea with a grin.

"Fair enough," says Officer Seth, "but I'm driving home!"

What else does Officer Seth do?

Directs traffic.

Helps investigate crime scenes.

Teaches children about safety.

Arrests criminals.

What does Officer Seth need?

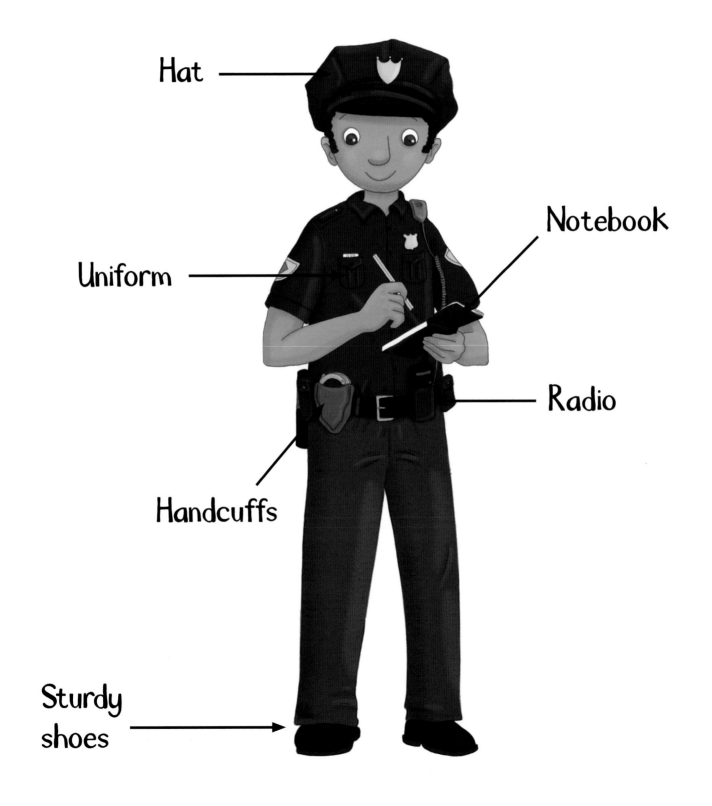

Hat

Notebook

Uniform

Radio

Handcuffs

Sturdy
shoes

Other busy people

Here are some of the other busy people police officers work with.

Police sergeants run the police station, managing the police officers and coordinating teams on investigations.

Forensic scientists examine evidence from crime scenes, including photographs, fingerprints, and samples.

Police dog handlers use highly trained dogs to help them find evidence at a crime scene.

Family liaison officers work with families affected by crime or an accident. An officer suppports the family and tells them what is happening.

Next steps

- Alex got separated from his mom and dad at the festival. Have you ever lost the person looking after you? Were you scared? What did you do?

- Alex found a police officer when he was lost. What did the police officer ask him for? Do you know what to do if you get lost?

- Officer Seth was on patrol at the festival. Ask the children why the police were there and what jobs they had to do at the festival.

- The police have wide and varied roles. Discuss these roles with the children and ask them why they are important. Ask them to imagine what would happen if there was no police force.

- Discuss the other jobs in the police force and what the children think about these roles. Would the children like to become police officers one day or work for the police? Which job would the children like to do most?

Publisher: Maxime Boucknooghe
Editorial Director: Victoria Garrard
Art Director: Miranda Snow
Editor: Sophie Hallam
Designer: Victoria Kimonidou
Consultant: Officer Yvonne Monaghan

Copyright © QEB Publishing 2016

First published in the United States by
QEB Publishing, Inc.
6 Orchard
Lake Forest, CA 92630

www.qed-publishing.co.uk

A catalog record for this book is available from the Library of Congress.

ISBN 978 1 60992 942 8

Printed in China

For Granny Wilson

- AndoTwin

For Mitchell & Rhys

- Lucy M. George